T0380740

The Book
of
Sayings

To order additional copies of this book, contact:
Xlibris
844-714-8691
www.Xlibris.com
Orders@Xlibris.com

ISBN: 979-8-3694-0458-4 (sc)
ISBN: 979-8-3694-0457-7 (e)

Library of Congress Control Number: 2023914319

Print information available on the last page

Rev. date: 04/29/2024

Table of Contents

The Book
of
Sayings

1) God is the light at the end of a dark tunnel; He always tries to guide you in the right direction, even if you choose not to see it.

2) True love never fades just because one ages.

3) The scars of life will only make you stronger in the end.

4) Nothing is promised, so don't expect everything you want to happen.

5) Material will burn, and your flesh will fade, but your soul will remain past the end of days.

6) Let your light shine, for darkness will never have its day.

7) Reading wisdom is similar to sipping wine; you can only take in so much at a time.

8) Let them hate me, for I know what makes me.

9) I'm a positive man living in a negative world.

10) Those who only look to take will have nothing; those that give in the end will be the ones receiving.

11) Water purifies the body like the truth purifies our souls.

12) Life is an investment; you get what you put into it.

13) A sincere person will tell you what is wrong while a deceitful person will watch you fall.

14) The composition of a person is the circumference of that which they have overcome.

15) Knowledge is chosen like the food we eat; we only accept what we're willing to take in.

16) The sun reflects off water like God reflects His will onto the Holy Spirit.

17) Scissors will cut through paper like the truth spoken cuts out the lies.

18) Rewarded is the man that makes the best of his life.

19) The fake will fade, and the real will continue to exist.

20) Inspiration is like a coin being dropped into a well; the insight of life is projected to encourage the mind to be hopeful.

21) The knife of betrayal is driven by those who are closest to us.

22) Soil fertilizes the earth like love enriches our hearts.

23) Height isn't anything but a few inches off the ground, and volume is nothing more than space taken.

24) You can't be genuine with anyone if you don't know yourself.

25) Like skipping stones on a lake, you take yourself in life as far as you want to go.

26) Pride, in the end, will lead to sorrow.

27) You can have the smarts, but it doesn't mean you have the will power.

28) A true partner is one who endures your pain.

29) When you cry, your tears wash away your sorrows.

30) It's better to be straightforward and let them know what is wrong than to hold it in and say nothing at all; in the long run, they will suffer from their own unnoticed internal issues.

31) The more you ignore, the less you come across.

32) You don't need money to feel equal to those who have it.

33) Without Jesus, Heaven would be far beyond man's reach.

34) The range of one's love starts at the gauge of one's heart.

35) Birds teach their young before they embark from the nest; this is how parents should teach and prepare their children for their journey into the world.

36) The insecure pass judgment because they're unstable in what they live for.

37) You can't go against who you are.

38) A person is similar to a drawing in the sand; as the times change, so does their picture.

39) Strength lies in a smile, not a frown.

40) Rain falling is similar to a teacher; the knowledge they have obtained is dispersed on to the students who live to absorb it.

41) Putting up a wall in life offers little protection; regardless of what you block out, life will continue to seep in.

42) Give love now because one day it might not be there.

43) You have to run as a soldier before you can walk like a general.

44) The world is similar to a lumberjack; those who stand alone are the ones they yearn to chop down.

45) The nucleus of an atom is similar to God; He is the eternal core to our universe.

46) All people have flaws in life, but it's up to each person to uproot them.

47) You can't prove nothing if it's not there.

48) If you're not content with yourself, you will never be satisfied with those around you.

49) The sacrifice is temporary, for your eternal reward in the end.

50) No matter how much you try to make your life sparkle, someone will always try to find dust on the other side.

12

51) People of the world will pass, but those who live for God will live on.

52) Just because you're old doesn't mean you've grown.

53) If the world can't control you, it desires to see your demise.

54) The only way to see how good you are is to test your abilities.

55) A compass is similar to the Bible; it navigates you through life, providing everlasting direction.

56) Faith is like a shield because it deflects the doubt from one's inclination.

57) You can't reason with those who have no sense.

58) Hate does not bring the true down, it only makes their resiliency stronger.

59) If you think you're above other people, it shows your level of ignorance.

60) Seeing your reflection within a passing stream is similar to having a clear conscious with God; His eyes are able to see clearly through you.

61) Spiritual energy can be released through one's passion.

62) Fake people are like glass because when the truth is heard, they break.

63) At one point in life, God will reach out to you, but you have to be willing to accept it.

64) Not every fish gets caught by the same bait.

65) True love is like a magnet; each one keeps the other from being separated.

66) The foreshadow of a person's heart is seen through their eyes.

67) You can't argue much when you know you're wrong.

68) When living the life of a lie, you have no path; you will always be led into false directions.

69) It's good to have a solid relationship with your family and friends.

70) When it comes to being open-minded, there's more life outside the box, so don't get stuck living in it.

71) The weather is unpredictable like the decisions made by fools.

72) In combat, get up when you have to, and stay down when you must.

73) You might have the experience, but God put you into the position.

74) Most people can always readily remember the bad things rather than the good things.

75) Every personality is a different form of culture; the more familiar you are with culture, the more familiar you'll be with people.

76) Every person is their own trinity through their mind, body, and spirit.

77) You can write for days, but if it has no meaning, it won't have any impact.

78) In sports, playing away games tests the effectiveness of your abilities.

79) Trash should be taken out like the removal of stress from one's life.

80) When we look across the ocean through the eyes, it appears endless, just as our thoughts can perceive our eternities.

81) It's easier to mold a person while they're young than try to convert them while their old.

82) Accepting Jesus in your life, in God's mind, is an everlasting memory.

83)   Being alone sometimes is the best way to see who you are.

84)   Don't talk down upon other's accomplishments when you fail to strive for your own.

85)   Perseverance is similar to light because no matter how much darkness is around, it will always overcome.

86)   Some people don't like to learn from others; they would prefer to learn by themselves.

87)   A chance is opportunity given; if they deserve it, don't be the one to take it away.

88)   Ignorance is like an ostrich because their head is grounded with no reason.

89)   Respect is honor; those that don't have it are a disgrace amongst the ones that do.

90)   Selfishness is similar to a bucket with holes; regardless of the efforts you pour forward, it will always empty out.

91)   A change of thought can provoke the mind.

92)   Every man doesn't need a team to accomplish his objectives.

93)   Progression in life is footsteps moved forward; don't allow people to make you walk back.

94)   Death is another step to another form of life.

95)   People who can conform are similar to clay; they are able to mold to fit the concept of their environment.

96)   You don't need to be a fighter to stand up against those who are strong.

97)   The giving of hope brings forth the daybreak of one's light.

98)   Meeting people in life is like walking down a hallway because each face you come across is different.

99)   Nosey people are similar to a fly; all they like to do is look around.

100)   Influence is like a rock being thrown into a pond; after the impact, it ripples persuasion across the paths that it touches.

101) Our bodies are temporary, and our souls are eternal; all we accomplish and strive for will determine the placement of our everlasting destinies.

102) In combat, the best way to attack your enemy is when you know their back is facing you.

103) You don't need a degree to be educated.

104) Those who look beyond your problems are willing to stick with you.

105) An egocentric person is similar to a reflection in the mirror; all they are able to look at is themselves.

106) A powerful spirit is one who searches beyond the limits of that which has been presented before them.

107) When you are confused within yourself, you're prone to mislead those who are around you.

108) When facing the power of God, all people will be humbled by His presence.

109) Having versatility in life is what gives you the edge.

110) A snob is similar to a peacock; if their materialistic spectacle is taken away, they will have nothing left to show.

111) If given no opportunity, one cannot prove oneself.

112) It's the parents that teach their children the way of life, but it's up to the children that become adults to choose their own way of living.

113) Hypocrites are similar to a chameleon; they can never stay true to their color.

114) Our life is music; the experiences we go through are the footnotes that are played from within it.

115) A person that talks down upon others is like a dog with rabies; you never know when they're ready to fully turn on you.

116) Some people feel good only when they are satisfied.

117) I don't have to act a certain way because I am who I am.

118) When you chase after lies, you end up nowhere.

119) Some people expect too much from the little amount they give.

120) Determination is similar to the durability of metals; each person can withstand so much intensity before they're capable to break.

121) The world condemns the people who are good and uplifts the people who are evil.

122) Have pride in the sense of improving yourself, but be humble to learn new things.

123) Your ethnicity doesn't make you superior to anyone; you will always be human.

124) You have to be a person of reason, not just a person of want.

125) A person who lusts over one's partner is like a jackal; when you step away, they're going to make an attempt to step in.

126) In life, while walking with God, we are filled with His honor through our struggles and accomplishments.

127) Don't underestimate anyone because their standards may surpass your expectations.

128) You shouldn't have to cheat on your partner to show you're no longer interested.

129) People are like a novel or a coloring book when it comes to their life and experiences.

130) The rotation of a clock dial is similar to those who are promiscuous; every person they come across is a different number.

131) Inconsideration is an apple that sits alone, rotting away within itself.

132) A person who only takes is like a desert; in the end, all they will do is dry you up.

133) Without being put through trials, you'll never learn.

134) Having a foundation for who you are is the key; everything else afterward is secondary.

135) A fisher bobber is similar to being carefree; you float through life freely, waiting for an opportunity to pull at you.

136) The world is a face, and the people are the blemishes that make it look ugly.

137) You can't wake someone up in life if they're stuck sleeping within it.

138) You don't need the lime light to know that you're a star.

139) Like lifting weights, resistance makes you stronger.

140) Curiosity is similar to looking through a telescope; you ponder upon the wonders that are displayed, but never attempting to connect the vision of life missing within yourself.

141) To avoid argument or scuffle, sometimes it's best just to let it go.

142) In the game of life, whether I hear boos or cheers, I will always be motivated to produce.

143) Good memories are like hidden treasure; they are always waiting to be dug up.

144) Block the shots that try to deter your own well-being.

145) A person who is narrow-minded is similar to a pipe because their motives only move in one direction.

146) You can only pretend to be someone you're not till someone realizes who you are.

147) Some people in life feel like they have to carry the weight of others to go further.

148) What you accomplish with your life will separate you from other people.

149) Many people in life have distaste for that which they cannot have.

150) A role model is similar to a sculpture; each one is defined by those who marvel upon their meaning.

151) How open-minded you are is how flexible you'll be.

152) Share what you have, even if you feel like you have nothing left to give.

153) Many individuals in life are underrated for the efforts they make.

154) When it comes to finding true love, you shouldn't have to keep telling someone how you feel; if they feel the same way, they will tell you too.

155) The hard-hearted are similar to cactus; they prick the hands of those who reach out to touch them.

156) Anyone can be an enlistee, but few are soldiers.

157) If you can't control the mind, you can't control the body.

158) Through all of our struggles, there is an outcome.

159) The biggest mistakes are made on our own.

160) Passion is shown like the beauty of a blooming flower; each one displays the aura that depicts from within.

161) Life is temporary, so make your time count.

162) A partner is not a need, it comes naturally.

163) A person of many colors is a picture that should be framed.

164) Time taken away can never be given back.

165) A person who lives for negativity is like a black hole; their inner conflict will deteriorate their physical being.

166) No matter how much you cut me off, I will always come through.

167) Like a log added to a fire, a good laugh will brighten someone's day.

168) Real men take care of their responsibilities.

169) Seek to preserve the ways of truth and peace.

170) A fishnet is similar to the bandwagon; it encircles those with deceit by wrapping them within their own demise.

171) True love will always support you and maintain a strong relationship.

172) The devil is similar to gravity; all through life, he tries holding you down.

173) When the truth is spoken among those who deny it, physically they appear normal, internally they will be startled.

174) Sometimes, you need to cut things out to make your life right.

175) A person who is easily aggravated is like dynamite; anytime their fuse is burned out, they are ready to explode.

176) Applying past experiences to the present mind builds fortitude toward your future outcome.

177) Just because someone acts hard doesn't make them strong.

178) If you deny the truth, you will constantly walk through life in circles.

179) Don't take advantage of those who lack self-control in taking care of themselves.

180) Defiance is like throwing a ball against a wall; no matter how much truth you've ignored, it will always bounce back to enlighten you in the end.

181) The word of God spoken will strike the enemy.

182) If it's always about you, you'll never learn anything new.

183) Just because you have position in life doesn't mean you will be satisfied.

184) You might have all the possessions but still have emptiness inside.

185) Passiveness is similar to sand on the beach; you don't mind being walked upon.

186) When it comes to fighting, real men fight as one, but cowards must fight in groups.

187) You can't keep chasing after someone if they keep running away.

188) All people have conflict; if one minor incident of conflict ends a relationship, the relationship was never meant to begin with.

189) Just because everything around you is widely accepted doesn't mean that it's right for you.

190) Corruption is similar to oil being poured into water; they've degraded those contacted by polluting the environments they have touched.

191) True love is like viewing the treetops of a forest; through our eyes it has no end.

192) When you try to do something good, the majority will oppose you.

193) A black patch over one's eye is similar to backsliders; one eye can see the light, and the other prefers the darkness of our world.

194) If a person does not support you, they're not worth your time.

195) A liar is similar to stacked dominos; each lie repeats a pattern, allowing one touch of truth to topple them down and fall.

196) Chances in life are given by the people we meet.

197) Everyone is a living destiny of which they have been sent to finish.

198) Positive names should be remembered; the negative ones should be swept away.

199) God wouldn't have given us eternal life if He didn't think we were capable.

200) Every person in life is like a walking collage; each person has different experiences that resemble the pictures and images that are depicted within them.

201) The design of evil is to create a mirage of all pleasures, blinding each victim from realizing the possible future of their everlasting suffering.

202) People who can't respect you don't have to be a part of your life.

203) Having ambition in life will help you over any obstacle that blocks your path.

204) Inspire those who need uplifting.

205) The devil is similar to a spider; he welcomes all of those who are spiritually blind, to be entangled into his infernal web.

206) The unwilling are never ready to sacrifice.

207) You can change the probable from happening.

208) Improvement comes with sacrifice.

209) Don't allow your spouse or partner to control your principles of living.

210) With a blank stare you walk through life, yearning for empty desires that will never supersede the spirit of God.

211) You shouldn't spoil someone just to keep them liking you.

212) You can't stop smoking if your living in fire.

213) When you have common courtesy, it shows your degree of respect.

214) No matter how beautiful someone is, they will never compare to your true love.

215) A piggy bank is similar to revelations; the sins of the world are stored away, amounting to the fulfillment of its own destruction.

216) Your spirit is a fortress; don't allow the enemy to smash through it.

217) Fame is like a light bulb because after your splendor is gone, you burn out.

218) God is the antidote to cure us from the poison of our world.

219) Few eyes go deeper than what they appear.

220) A pack of hyenas are similar to demons; they find their fools and laugh while they finish them as prey.

221) My inner power comes from the support of God.

222) If people were satisfied with themselves, they would be more content with the world around them.

223)   You can't manipulate anyone if no one is around.

224)   When you deny the truth, you neglect the council of God.

225)   Sin is similar to poison; it stimulates the flesh by slowly deteriorating our inner being.

226)   Don't force yourself into a relationship just to make others happy; the only one who is going to end up unhappy is you.

227)   You can come back from what you have lost.

228)   Dirt is the foundation of the earth like God is the foundation to our Universe.

229)   Do what your income can sustain.

230)   A person who looks at others in a relationship is similar to a windmill; their head turns to the direction of those passing.

231)   Everyone wants answers, but very few seek the truth.

232)   Life is given to you for a reason, but it's up to you to fulfill your purpose.

233)   Situations in life happen at moments we don't expect; what we gain from them is what makes us stronger in the end.

234) You can't tease if no one wants to play.

235) Persecution is similar to a hurricane; suffering is imposed destructively onto those that don't want it.

236) If you love God and love others, your life will maintain balance.

237) Those that make people suffer will end up suffering themselves.

238) Some people will never be satisfied with who they are.

239) Nothing should stop you from enjoying your life.

240) Those who live for the world are slowly burning until the end when they have become one with the ashes.

241) Don't stab your enemy unless you know you're ready for battle.

242) The first battle can be lost, but the second can still be won.

243) When you put yourself in God's hands, He takes care of you.

244) A good artist always comes out with new forms of expression.

245) A person who is confused is similar to a spinning vinyl record; if they're not pointed in the right direction, they will move through life in circles.

246) Just because people are friendly doesn't make them weak.

247) The war of life is relentless, but those who keep striving will prevail.

248) Having a variety of true friends in life allows us to build new characteristics to improve and strengthen our well-being.

249) Within most governments of the world, there is much talk and little reform.

250) Those who live in sin are like smoke because they remain in life for a suspended moment in time, afterward never seeing them again.

251) The wind is similar to the soul; it progresses and transgresses freely.

252) Many people settle for what they already have, never seeking to accomplish more.

253) Regardless if one or many neglect you, never let them hold back your potential.

254) The truth fortifies your life while lies pacify your destruction.

255) A person of greed is similar to a pig; no matter how much material they've consumed, they never will be satisfied.

256) In life, the path is only found by those who are willing to look for it.

257) Recognition comes from within.

258) Like the construction of a house, your life is built up in the manner you choose to make it.

259) Life and death are both new experiences each of us must face.

260) Satan is similar to a man smoking a cigar; all people who live in sin are flicked into his burning ashtray.

261) Don't be ashamed of who you are.

262) When content with yourself, look to uplift the well-being of those who are around you.

263) The truth is natural like the elements of the earth.

264) When you involve your life with only one person, you miss out on everyone else around you.

265) Shallowness is like a vase; their beauty is only temporary through the items they live to uphold.

266) Most government leaders don't amount to their position.

267) A child having a tantrum is similar to an attitude; both throw a fit when they don't get their way.

268) A person who lives for material will stand for nothing if all they have is taken away.

269) When you're fixed into one setting, you miss the big picture.

270) A dog has no conscience, like a person who cheats on their partner has no shame.

271) Every empire that man has constructed throughout time has fallen.

272) Those that can completely think for themselves can embrace free will.

273) Air and water maintain life on earth; take care of them.

274) You can't build a relationship off one person.

275) Fools are similar to plankton; they follow in large masses to be deceitfully consumed.

276) Stand above those who attempt to bring you down.

277) Gossip is for the weak-minded and insecure, by passing false judgment upon others to temporarily pacify their own weaknesses.

278) Life glorifies the chance to perform or accomplish anything your body and mind have accepted and can adapt to.

279) You don't need handshakes or appraisals to feel good about yourself.

280) Evil is similar to a school of piranhas; when you thrive for the pleasures of the flesh, they will be drawn to rip you apart.

281) Don't jump into the situation till you realize what's going on.

282) Pride is like a balloon that floats alone, ready to be popped.

283) In combat, hit your enemy hard, or don't hit them at all.

284) Do what you want with what you're given.

285) Flies circling around manure is similar to drama; most people want their piece of the pile.

286) The eyes are the closest way to depict one's motive in thinking.

287) Negativity is a form of insecurity that puts others down so that one can feel upright.

288) Understanding the concept outlines the perspective.

289) No matter how much you try to connect with the world, it will never connect with you.

290) Vanity is like a statue; they vision all people as spectators marveling upon themselves.

291) The difference between each soul is the ones who are defined.

292) Some people's lives are handed to them, while others have to earn it.

293) Morals are manifested by those who live to embrace them.

294) True strength lies in being direct.

295) Artillery fire is similar to someone who is critical; they barrage complaints about everything within their area.

296) People have doubt in each other, and doubt is a weakness, but having faith symbolizes the ability to believe.

297) Once you know who you are, everything you go through will be cornerstones added to the pyramid of your life.

298) The truth is like a sword; it will rip through you.

299) A constant negative outlook on life, in time, will drain your body's life force.

300) Evil eats each victim till there's nothing left for them to chew; after they have finished, they throw away all those who were used.

301) God is similar to a farmer; He plants and sows the seeds of eternal life for those that will bring forth His everlasting harvest.

302) Happiness brings you inner life, while sorrow takes it away.

303) I don't need anything the world has to offer me; all I need is what I've earned on my own.

304) Every trial we go through adds an extra piece of armor to fortify our hearts and minds.

305) A wise man is similar to an archer; he perceives past the deceit, and when he speaks, his precision of words will pierce through you.

306) How you treat people in life as a whole is how you'll be treated in the end.

307) It's good to be observant but not judgmental.

308) Everything new you see adds color throughout the big picture of your life.

309) It's not about the author, it's what they have written.

310) A cool breeze on a hot day is similar to the spirit of God; when our hearts are troubled, he unexpectedly comforts the pain.

311) Going through evil has strengthened me to do good.

312) If you take your time constructing the outcome, the end results will be more efficient.

313) Having self-confidence is a continuous reinforcement of your inner being.

314) Negativity can make you fight harder for what you believe in.

315) Always be proud of what you have, and never be ashamed of that you have been given.

316) You don't need to involve the world into your relationship.

317) It's good to train your fist even though there is peace.

318) Do not allow people with misleading concepts to obscure your perception.

319) Reaping benefits in life depends on how hard you're willing to work.

320) Whispers are faint sounds; you can only hear God if your open to His calling.

321) If anyone betrays you, it shows the quality of their loyalty.

322) Most people think once they've learned something, they know it all.

323) Have compassion for those who need your attention.

324) Regardless if you have no support, you will always have yourself.

325) God is similar to a waterfall; He pours forth His love, uplifting those who drink the water of everlasting life.

326) Don't steal from anyone; what you have is what you've gained on your own.

327) The prosperity of good means the desolation to all that is evil.

328) True friends treat you as an ally, not an enemy.

329) Life is a journey toward your everlasting destination.

330) Discipline should be instilled into all children; without discipline, those same children will become adults that will not care to separate the differences between what is right and what is wrong.

331) Just because you're a symbol of status does not make you above other people.

332) People who are self-serving are leeches amongst the world.

333) When it comes to a relationship, you should accept the person for who they are, not what you want them to become.

334) A hollow heart lacks compassion for those who are in pain.

335) The word of God is similar to drinking water; it keeps us healthy by hydrating our souls.

336) Size does not matter when determination can bring down the height or weight of your opponent.

337) Friends that stop talking to you after finding a relationship were never real friends to begin with.

338) Regardless of what you know, there is always something else to pick up.

339) Don't start a family where it doesn't belong.

340) God's name spoken is similar to a screeching chalkboard; every time His name is uttered, evil will cringe to His name.

341) A strong soul can pierce the eyes of the weak-minded.

342) You can't say you've come up if everything was handed to you.

343) If you don't teach your kids how to take hits in life, they will have a difficult time recovering from them while growing up.

344) The giving of a few can change the hearts of many.

345) Forgiveness is similar to a rug; before entering the house of God, your sins must be wiped away.

346) Strategy increases the efficiency in completing the objective.

347) The family that is there are the ones who care.

348) Attack your fears.

349) True concepts fade away false deceptions.

350) The truth cuts your eternal being like a piece of fruit; it cuts out the bad parts and preserves the rest.

351) Just because you don't have the numbers doesn't mean your team can't win.

352) All people, given life, get a chance to live; only few will live beyond their existence.

353) No matter how many people you know, you'll never be capable of understanding them all.

354) Being able to make others laugh or smile is a God-given gift.

355) The amount of effort put toward healing shows the quality of one's compassion.

356) Don't try to impress anyone; let them like you for who you are.

357) A real person breaks down fake people like a lawnmower does to grass.

358) Life is unequal, so each person sets their own balance.

359) A positive personality can bring the brightest light upon the darkest days.

360) The Trinity is similar to an arrowhead; Jesus and the Holy Spirit stand on each side supporting God, the everlasting centerpiece.

361) Your inside will hide many faces, but your outside will only show one.

362) Life is not given to you just because you have money in your pocket.

363) The Lantern of Salvation shines divinity throughout the darkness of our world.

364) Soldiers and civil servants do the jobs that civilians aren't willing to do.

365) Long-distance relationships between a couple test the amount of loyalty and devotion by both partners, by showing if each partner can endure in the relationship without the other physically being there.

366) Second-guessing yourself can increase your failure.

367) Regardless if the Bible is written by man, the message is still directed from God.

368) Trials can make you stronger only if you don't allow them to overcome you.

369) When you neglect God, you fail to recognize your everlasting opportunity.

370) Youth can learn from the experience of age, and age can learn from the fruitfulness of youth.

371) Knowledge is deep, but wisdom is deeper.

372) Being neglected is not a loss; it's poor decision making by others in not realizing your full potential.

373) When someone's eyes always look upon the ground, their confidence doesn't serve them.

374) Certain people that don't express themselves have hidden agendas.

375) True love will walk till the end of their time, without attempting to be separated.

376) Hell is like a dumpster; all the trash of the world is thrown into it.

377) There will be rough times throughout life; use positive thoughts to refortify your mind.

378) A true government upholds the view of its people by improving their ways of living.

379) Every day of life is a continuing fulfillment of your existence.

380) The vines of a vineyard stretch across the land; like God, His hand reaches out to all those He can.

381) Love can only be if two beings share the same devotion and loyalty to one another.

382) The fog deters your vision like false testimony obstructs your mind.

383) A good leader knows his soldiers and recognizes their capabilities.

384) A hermit is similar to a snail; they only come out from their shell when they have to.

385) In combat, horsemen are swift on the battlefield; similar to Angels, they attack with fury past the eyes that are unable to see.

386) The people who envy are the ones that are dissatisfied with their lives.

387) God does not bless those who are corrupt.

388) When alone and faltering, a good brotherhood will keep a man together.

389) The Holy Spirit embraces all those who are willing to listen.

390) A good church that follows the word of God is similar to a hospital; it brings spiritual health amongst their people.

391) The wise will try to improve the weaknesses they see in others.

392) When around people, don't be afraid to express yourself.

393) Absorb life's energy to make yourself complete.

394) I have learned from the greatest minds that have experienced living in time.

395) A prestigious person might have title in the world, but stand for nothing facing the eyes of God.

396) The devil will employ anything for you to unfulfill your purpose.

397) There's no trash to be dished out when it's already been dumped.

398) You can't keep reaching out to somebody if they don't want to reach out to you.

399) I am who I am based on personality, not by a picture.

400) God is similar to a blacksmith; the people that are chosen are molded through life as tools to serve Him.

401) Good and evil are playing darts; our world is their board, and each target determines the value of their influence.

402) Like fire in a dark tunnel, when you find true love, it will lighten up your heart.

403) You benefit from those who are willing to support your outcome.

404) When you believe, you see beyond what others don't know.

405) Those that can adapt are similar to clouds; they're able to fluctuate and adjust to the atmosphere of their surroundings.

406) False confidence is similar to a firework because after their front is displayed it's gone.

407) The body is similar to a tire; life slowly breaks you down to complete the circle of your life.

408) Having emotion is the first step to feeling your spirit.

409) Being self-sufficient is more reliable than being dependent.

410) Asking God for His forgiveness is similar to bathing; He washes away the sins that you have committed.

411) I do not need to flex to know that I am strong.

412) Many people disguise themselves to keep their true motives hidden.

413) A faithful partner is one who will stand by you, regardless of the temptations that are presented before them.

414) Adapting is one of the best abilities to help you overcome various situations that you may face throughout your life.

415) Autumn leaves falling are similar to comments; there's always plenty to give out, but in the end, they amount to nothing.

416) Your mind is not a puddle, don't let everyone splash into it.

417) Most people don't want to see you happier than what they're feeling for themselves.

418) When people are caught up in their life, they tend to pass on everyone else's.

419) When you're with someone you love, you don't need anyone else.

420) Dead trees lacked water and sunlight; like a person without knowledge or wisdom, they will dwindle away.

421) Fools accept all that's before them, but the wise will perceive past the deceptions.

422) Very few want to see you come up, and almost all want to see you fall.

423) Giving people represent the oases throughout the gluttony of the desert in our world.

424) Like kerosene to a fire, your soul keeps you glowing.

425) A dominating person is similar to a wolverine; it's in their nature to overpower the people they come across.

426) The world has a one set mind to fulfill its own destruction.

427) All those that love God and serve Him will be leaves upon the tree of life.

428) Experience using the spiritual energies that are within you.

429) A good soul can answer for itself.

430) A person that is stressed is similar to earthquakes; those who hold their tension look for ways to release the pressure.

431) Christians are similar to camels; they store the knowledge and wisdom of God through the world's desert.

432) The weak-minded can't think for themselves.

433) Forgetting means walking back over your own footprints.

434) If you turn your back on a true friend, more backs in time will be turned towards you.

435) An anxious person is similar to a hummingbird, they're unable to sit still in one place.

436) All those who stand against God will fall.

437) Listen to all perspectives before considering yours is the only one.

438) Our spirit fortifies our state of being.

439) Revenge will never amount to the damage that was caused; that which was done has already been finished.

440) Life is similar to a phone call at a payphone; as you speak, your life is explained, and the change that is entered signifies the years that you've spent.

441) In the end, what I realized and what I overcame is that I have become.

442) If all choose to fall around you, don't lay with them.

443) God gives you life while satan attempts to take it away.

441) When it comes to friends, you only want the flowers and grass in your garden, not the weeds.

445) Men go to war to fight for their country, but when they fight in battles, they do not fight for their country; what they do fight for is their own survival and the survival of their fellow soldiers.

446) When it comes to people, solids stick together, and liquids separate.

447) Hate is like a disease; it will consume you.

448) If you're selfish in any relationship, in time, you might end up alone.

449) Always continue to refresh your mind with what you already know.

450) A person who is uncertain is like a child on a swing; no matter how much you push them forward, they will always sway back and forth in the same direction.

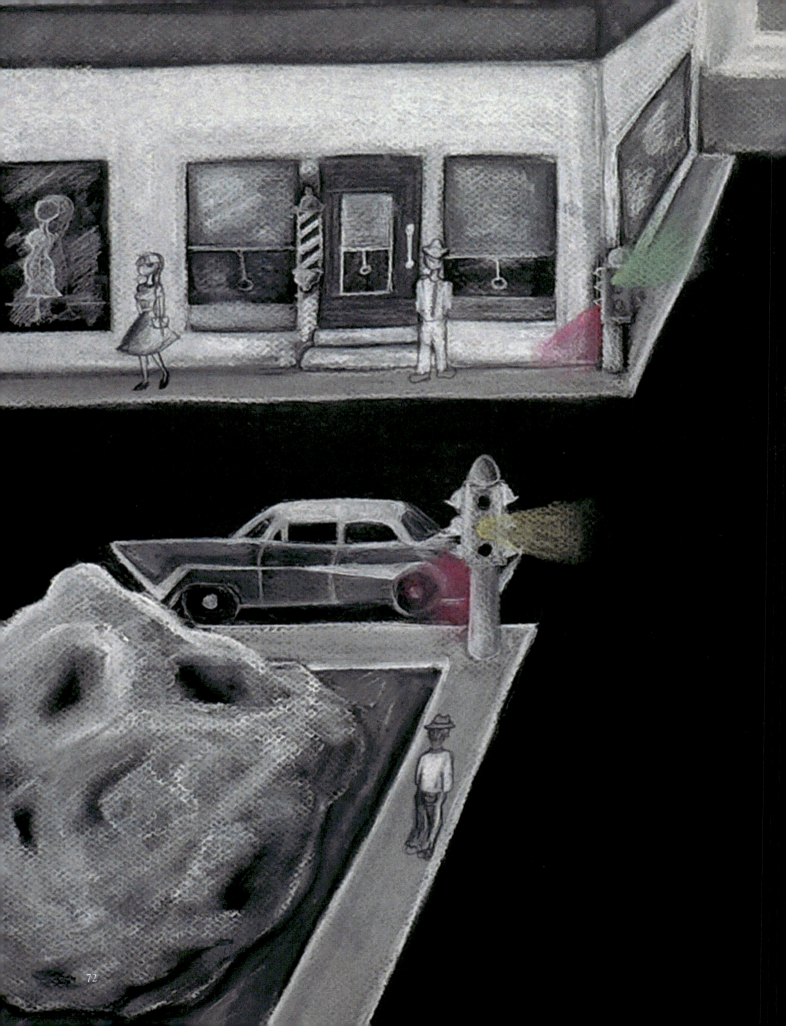

451) People's continuous mishaps lead to their downfalls.

452) Always be real, even if everyone else around you is fake.

453) Learn from your mistakes because in the end they will only have strengthened you.

454) Don't grieve for death, for those that have passed want you to accomplish all and more in what they were never able to achieve.

455) Knowledge is similar to exploring; regardless of how much you've obtained, you can always attempt to go further.

456) It's good to change scenery in the things we do.

457) After death, the soul is the remnant of our minds and bodies.

458) You get out of life what you're willing to absorb from it.

459) Your eyes are only open to what you're willing to see.

460) The quilt is sewn, stitching together each seam; like life, its put together in segments, fulfilling the design of one's time.

461) Peace will come to men when all men have realized there is no need to harm one another.

462) It's the big things we try to accomplish, but the little things that can hold us down.

463) If you borrow money, be responsible and take the initiative to pay it back.

464) Life is an honor, and you're the one who lives to honor it.

465) Depression is similar to a faltering bridge; if the footsteps of stress are constantly applied, you will break down and fall.

466) When you live for the view of others, you fail to recognize your own identity.

467) The dedication of two hearts brings together one mind.

468) If you can't get past the basics, you'll never advance.

469) Sometimes, the best peace of life is complete relaxation.

470) Armageddon is similar to the Civil War; all have chosen their everlasting federation, amounting to the final outcome of eternal war.

471) When you hate life, everything around you is stale.

472) The mind is like a forest because we allow the atmosphere to harbor inside.

473) Don't hold on to anything that isn't there.

474) Accepting the corruption of the world will bring death to your soul.

475) Love is like glue; it sticks to those who appreciate it by keeping them together.

476) Countries and teams wear colors that symbolize what they stand for; our colors fly within our hearts.

477) A safe is similar to potential; it remains sealed until you figure out the possibilities of what's inside.

478) Release your energy, don't hold it in.

479) If God has given you a gift, don't deny yourself and those you might be able to help by not using it.

480) Life is similar to an hourglass; you try to squeeze everything in before your time runs out.

481) Having a companion is similar to a pillow; the comfort in having one can relax your mind through soothing you.

482) The progress of technology advertises the diminishing of humanity.

483) Those who live to hurt others in life will spend their eternities in everlasting terror.

484) You might start out ahead in life, but it does not mean that you will finish first.

485)	Life is similar to an empty bag; the items that are inserted signify the contents of our experiences.

486)	The soldier makes the rank, the rank doesn't make the soldier.

487)	After you find yourself, no one can change you.

488)	The Lord gives me my strength to accomplish my objectives.

489)	Only people that are involved in drama like to cause scenes in public.

490)	Your mind is similar to your stomach; no matter how much you have obtained, you will never be fulfilled.

491)	Perseverance is the doorstep to achievement.

492)	Age does not set the level of one's description.

493)	People will say they care, but only few will truly mean it.

494)	In the end, you can't blame God or the devil for what you've become.

495)	Hatred is like viruses; the more you come across in time, the more you will become immune to.

496)	When it comes to self-improvement in life, it's like eating at a banquet; you pick the good qualities, and you get rid of the rest.

497) Be your own person, don't live for the lies and deceit of the world.

498) Don't move if you want to be touched.

499) Life is but a second of your eternity.

500) In life, God and satan are playing a game of chess; during life, you've chosen the affiliation and the significance of your piece.

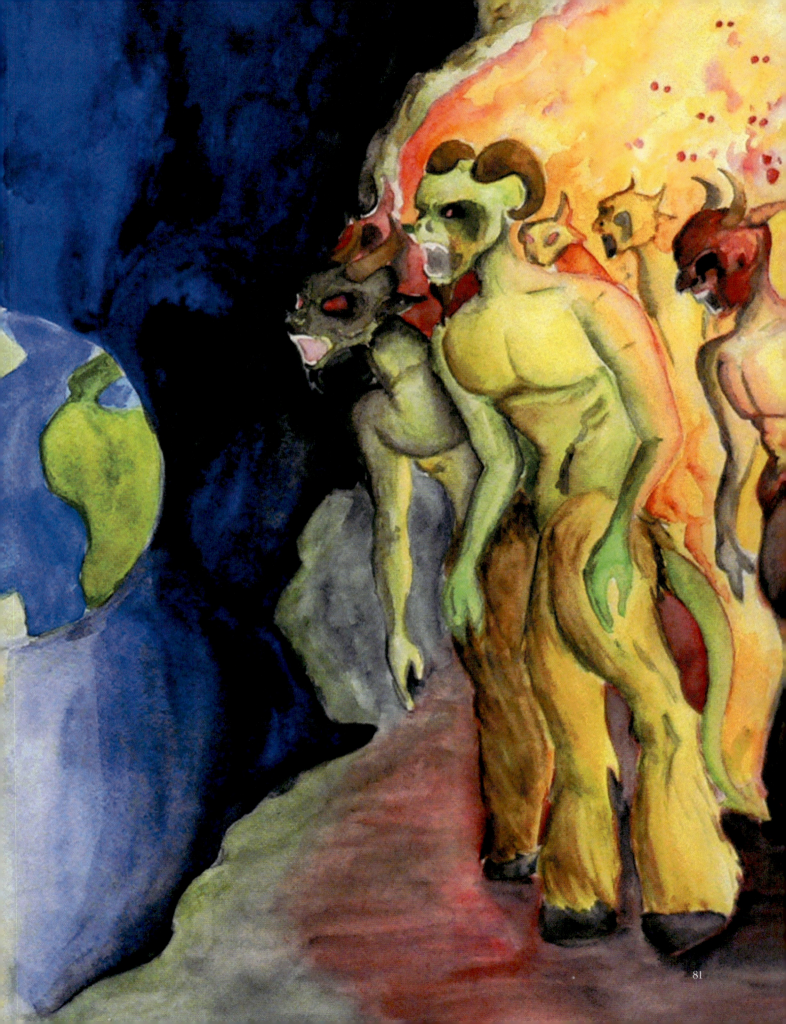

Special Thanks:

To God for giving me life and allowing me to become who I am,
my grandparents for always being there and supporting me,
my father and mother for raising me and teaching me,
my family who truly supported me, my true friends, thank you
Rachel Guzman for the artwork, you did a wonderful work,
and photographer Mindy Le Jeune. Also, to all the good people,
acquaintances, random encounters who supported me
and inspired me through various moments of my life.
Above all, thanks again to God.

If you like this book, you may also check other books author has written:

The Color of Wisdom
Visions of Reason
Arts of Truth
The Ant Who Found The Truth